THE WONDERFUL WIZARD OF OZ

VOL. 3

ADAPTED FROM THE NOVEL BY L. FRANK BAUM

Writer: ERIC SHANOWER
Artist: SKOTTIE YOUNG
Colorist: JEAN-FRANCOIS BEAULIEU
Letterer: JEFF ECKLEBERRY

Assistant Editors: LAUREN SANKOVITCH & LAUREN HENRY
Associate Editor: NATE COSBY
Senior Editor: RALPH MACCHIO

Special Thanks to Chris Allo, Rich Ginter, Jeff Suter & Jim Nausedas
Collection Editor: MARK D. BEAZLEY
Assistant Editors: NELSON RIBEIRO & ALEX STARBUCK
Editor, Special Projects: JENNIFER GRÜNWALD
Senior Editor, Special Projects: JEFF YOUNGQUIST
SVP of Print & Digital Publishing Sales: DAVID GABRIEL
Production: JERRY KALINOWSKI
Book Design: SPRING HOTELING

Editor in Chief: AXEL ALONSO
Chief Creative Officer: JOE QUESADA
Publisher: DAN BUCKLEY
Executive Producer: ALAN FINE

MARVEL

visit us at www.abdopublishing.com

Reinforced library bound edition published in 2014 by Spotlight, a division of the ABDO Group, PO Box 398166, Minneapolis, Minnesota 55439. Spotlight produces high-quality reinforced library bound editions for schools and libraries. Published by agreement with Marvel Characters, Inc.

Printed in the United States of America, North Mankato, Minnesota.
102013
012014
♻ This book contains at least 10% recycled materials.

Marvel.com
© 2014 Marvel

Library of Congress Cataloging-in-Publication Data

Shanower, Eric.
  The wonderful Wizard of Oz / adapted from the novel by L. Frank Baum ; writer: Eric Shanower ; artist: Skottie Young. -- Reinforced library bound edition.
      pages cm
  "Marvel."
  Summary: An eight-volume, graphic novel adaptation of L. Frank Baum's tales of Dorothy, a little girl from Kansas who is blown by a storm to the magical land of Oz, where she has amazing adventures while trying to get home.
  ISBN 978-1-61479-226-0 (vol. 1) -- ISBN 978-1-61479-227-7 (vol. 2) -- ISBN 978-1-61479-228-4 (vol. 3) -- ISBN 978-1-61479-229-1 (vol. 4) -- ISBN 978-1-61479-230-7 (vol. 5) -- ISBN 978-1-61479-231-4 (vol. 6) -- ISBN 978-1-61479-232-1 (vol. 7) -- ISBN 978-1-61479-233-8 (vol. 8)
  1. Graphic novels. [1. Graphic novels. 2. Fantasy.] I. Young, Skottie, illustrator. II. Baum, L. Frank (Lyman Frank), 1856-1919. III. Title.
  PZ7.7.S453Won 2014
  741.5'973--dc23
                                    2013029128

All Spotlight books are reinforced library binding and manufactured in the United States of America.

THEY WERE OBLIGED TO CAMP OUT THAT NIGHT UNDER A LARGE TREE.

DOROTHY AND TOTO ATE THE LAST OF THEIR BREAD, AND NOW SHE DID NOT KNOW WHAT THEY WOULD DO FOR BREAKFAST.

IF YOU WISH, I'LL GO INTO THE FOREST AND KILL A DEER FOR YOU.

YOU CAN ROAST IT BY THE FIRE, SINCE YOUR TASTES ARE SO PECULIAR THAT YOU PREFER COOKED FOOD.

DON'T! PLEASE DON'T!

I SHOULD CERTAINLY WEEP IF YOU KILLED A POOR DEER, AND THEN MY JAWS WOULD RUST AGAIN.

BUT THE LION WENT AND FOUND HIS OWN SUPPER. NO ONE EVER KNEW WHAT IT WAS, FOR HE DIDN'T MENTION IT.

THE SCARECROW FOUND A TREE FULL OF NUTS.

YOU DROP ALMOST AS MANY AS YOU PUT IN THE BASKET!

I DON'T MIND HOW LONG IT TAKES, FOR IT ENABLES ME TO KEEP AWAY FROM THE FIRE.

THE SCARECROW ONLY CAME NEAR THE FLAMES TO COVER DOROTHY WITH DRY LEAVES WHEN SHE LAY DOWN TO SLEEP.

WHEN IT WAS DAYLIGHT, THE GIRL BATHED HER FACE IN A LITTLE RIPPLING BROOK, AND SOON AFTER THEY ALL STARTED TOWARD THE EMERALD CITY.

THEY HAD HARDLY BEEN WALKING AN HOUR WHEN --

WHAT SHALL WE DO?

I HAVEN'T THE FAINTEST IDEA.

WE CANNOT FLY, THAT'S CERTAIN. NEITHER CAN WE CLIMB DOWN INTO THIS GREAT DITCH. THEREFORE, IF WE CANNOT JUMP OVER IT, WE MUST STOP WHERE WE ARE.

I THINK *I* COULD JUMP OVER IT.

THEN WE'RE ALL RIGHT. YOU CAN CARRY US ALL OVER ON YOUR BACK, ONE AT A TIME.

I'M TERRIBLY AFRAID OF FALLING MYSELF, BUT I SUPPOSE THERE IS NOTHING TO DO BUT TRY IT.

WHO WILL GO FIRST?

I WILL, FOR IF YOU FOUND THAT YOU COULD NOT JUMP OVER, DOROTHY WOULD BE KILLED, OR THE TIN WOODMAN BADLY DENTED ON THE ROCKS BELOW.

BUT THE FALL WOULD NOT HURT *ME* AT ALL.

GET ON MY BACK AND WE'LL MAKE THE ATTEMPT.

WHY DON'T YOU RUN AND JUMP?

BECAUSE THAT ISN'T THE WAY WE LIONS DO THESE THINGS.

*T*HEY WERE ALL GREATLY PLEASED, AND THE LION SPRANG ACROSS THE DITCH AGAIN.

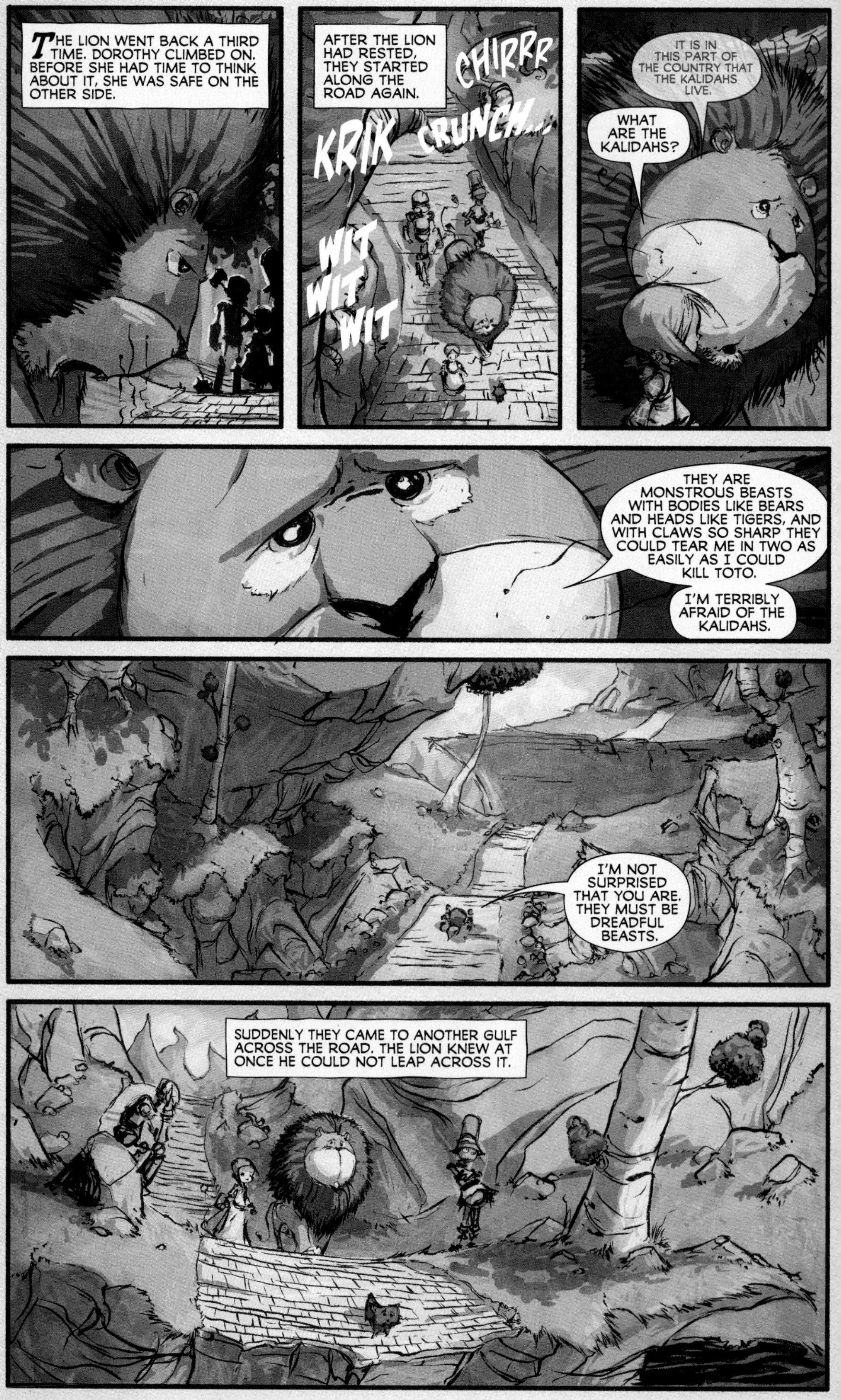
THE LION WENT BACK A THIRD TIME. DOROTHY CLIMBED ON. BEFORE SHE HAD TIME TO THINK ABOUT IT, SHE WAS SAFE ON THE OTHER SIDE.
AFTER THE LION HAD RESTED, THEY STARTED ALONG THE ROAD AGAIN.
CHIRRR
KRIK
CRUNCH...
WIT WIT WIT
IT IS IN THIS PART OF THE COUNTRY THAT THE KALIDAHS LIVE.
WHAT ARE THE KALIDAHS?
THEY ARE MONSTROUS BEASTS WITH BODIES LIKE BEARS AND HEADS LIKE TIGERS, AND WITH CLAWS SO SHARP THEY COULD TEAR ME IN TWO AS EASILY AS I COULD KILL TOTO.
I'M TERRIBLY AFRAID OF THE KALIDAHS.
I'M NOT SURPRISED THAT YOU ARE. THEY MUST BE DREADFUL BEASTS.
SUDDENLY THEY CAME TO ANOTHER GULF ACROSS THE ROAD. THE LION KNEW AT ONCE HE COULD NOT LEAP ACROSS IT.

IF THE TIN WOODMAN CAN CHOP THIS GREAT TREE DOWN, SO THAT IT WILL FALL TO THE OTHER SIDE, WE CAN WALK ACROSS IT EASILY.

THAT'S A FIRST RATE IDEA. ONE WOULD ALMOST SUSPECT YOU HAD BRAINS IN YOUR HEAD INSTEAD OF STRAW.

WHACK!

CRREEEEAK

CRRASH-SH-SH

...GRRRRRRRRRRRRRRAA!

QUICK! LET'S CROSS OVER!

THE KALIDAHS!

RROAAAHRR!

RUH?

RRR!

WE ARE LOST!

RRrAHH!

AHHRRR!

RAAAAHH!

THEY'LL SURELY TEAR US TO PIECES WITH THEIR SHARP CLAWS! BUT STAND CLOSE BEHIND ME AND I'LL FIGHT THEM AS LONG AS I'M ALIVE!

RAAARRR!

ROaRRR!

WAIT A MINUTE!

CHOP AWAY THE END OF THE TREE!

CHOK!

CRACK!

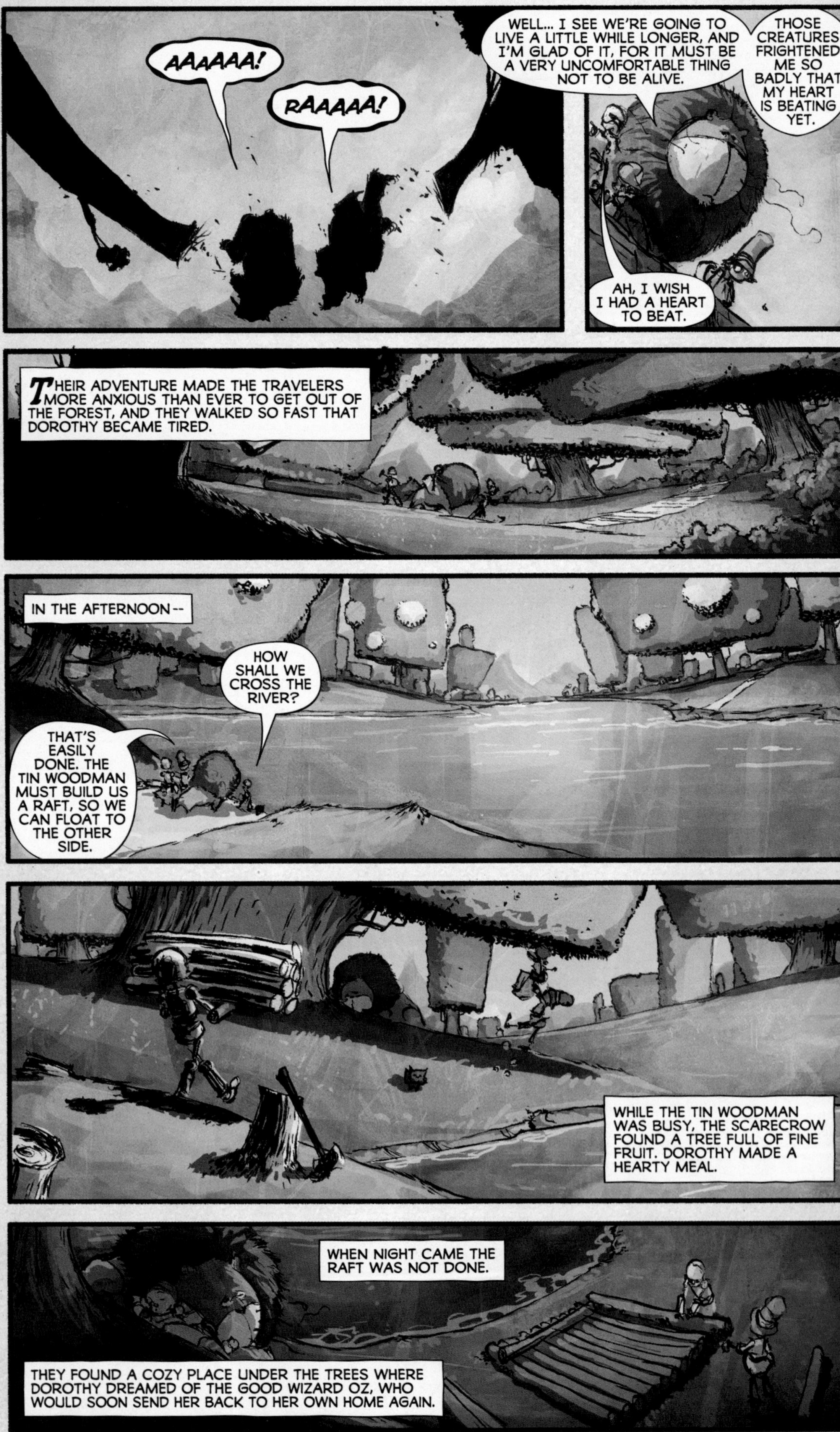
AAAAAA!
RAAAAA!
WELL... I SEE WE'RE GOING TO LIVE A LITTLE WHILE LONGER, AND I'M GLAD OF IT, FOR IT MUST BE A VERY UNCOMFORTABLE THING NOT TO BE ALIVE.
THOSE CREATURES FRIGHTENED ME SO BADLY THAT MY HEART IS BEATING YET.
AH, I WISH I HAD A HEART TO BEAT.
THEIR ADVENTURE MADE THE TRAVELERS MORE ANXIOUS THAN EVER TO GET OUT OF THE FOREST, AND THEY WALKED SO FAST THAT DOROTHY BECAME TIRED.
IN THE AFTERNOON--
HOW SHALL WE CROSS THE RIVER?
THAT'S EASILY DONE. THE TIN WOODMAN MUST BUILD US A RAFT, SO WE CAN FLOAT TO THE OTHER SIDE.
WHILE THE TIN WOODMAN WAS BUSY, THE SCARECROW FOUND A TREE FULL OF FINE FRUIT. DOROTHY MADE A HEARTY MEAL.
WHEN NIGHT CAME THE RAFT WAS NOT DONE.
THEY FOUND A COZY PLACE UNDER THE TREES WHERE DOROTHY DREAMED OF THE GOOD WIZARD OZ, WHO WOULD SOON SEND HER BACK TO HER OWN HOME AGAIN.

NEXT MORNING THEY AWAKENED REFRESHED AND FULL OF HOPE. ONLY THE RIVER NOW CUT THEM OFF FROM THE LOVELY, SUNNY COUNTRY THAT SEEMED TO BECKON THEM ON TO THE EMERALD CITY.

THEY GOT ALONG QUITE WELL AT FIRST...

...BUT WHEN THEY REACHED THE MIDDLE OF THE RIVER THE CURRENT SWEPT THE RAFT FARTHER AND FARTHER AWAY FROM THE ROAD OF YELLOW BRICK.

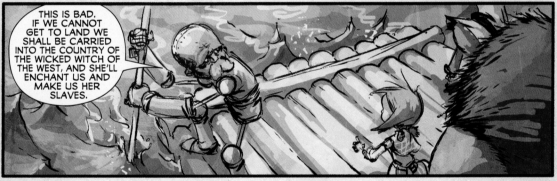

THIS IS BAD. IF WE CANNOT GET TO LAND WE SHALL BE CARRIED INTO THE COUNTRY OF THE WICKED WITCH OF THE WEST, AND SHE'LL ENCHANT US AND MAKE US HER SLAVES.

AND THEN I SHOULD GET NO BRAINS.

AND I SHOULD GET NO COURAGE.

AND I SHOULD GET NO HEART.

AND I SHOULD NEVER GET BACK TO KANSAS.

WE MUST CERTAINLY GET TO THE EMERALD CITY IF WE CAN!

OOOH --

GOOD-BYE!

SCARECROW!

*T*HE SCARECROW'S FRIENDS WERE VERY SORRY TO LEAVE HIM.

THE TIN WOODMAN BEGAN TO CRY, BUT REMEMBERED THAT HE MIGHT RUST, SO DRIED HIS TEARS ON DOROTHY'S APRON.

I'M NOW WORSE OFF THAN WHEN I FIRST MET DOROTHY.

THEN I WAS STUCK ON A POLE IN A CORNFIELD -- WHERE I COULD MAKE-BELIEVE SCARE THE CROWS, AT ANY RATE.

BUT SURELY THERE'S NO USE FOR A SCARECROW STUCK ON A POLE IN THE MIDDLE OF A RIVER.

I'M AFRAID I SHALL NEVER HAVE ANY BRAINS, AFTER ALL!

DOWN THE STREAM THE RAFT FLOATED, AND THE POOR SCARECROW WAS LEFT FAR BEHIND.

I THINK I CAN SWIM TO THE SHORE AND PULL THE RAFT AFTER ME...

...IF YOU'LL ONLY HOLD FAST TO THE TIP OF MY TAIL.

IT WAS HARD WORK, BUT BY AND BY THEY WERE DRAWN OUT OF THE CURRENT.

WHAT SHALL WE DO NOW?

WE MUST GET BACK TO THE ROAD, IN SOME WAY.

THE BEST PLAN WILL BE TO WALK ALONG THE RIVER BANK UNTIL WE COME TO THE ROAD AGAIN.

WHEN THEY WERE RESTED, THEY STARTED BACK TO THE ROAD.

IT WAS A LOVELY COUNTRY, AND HAD THEY NOT FELT SO SORRY FOR THE POOR SCARECROW, THEY COULD HAVE BEEN VERY HAPPY.

AFTER A TIME --

LOOK!

WHAT CAN WE DO TO SAVE HIM?

WHO ARE YOU, AND WHERE ARE YOU GOING?

I'M DOROTHY AND THESE ARE MY FRIENDS THE TIN WOODMAN AND THE COWARDLY LION. WE ARE GOING TO THE EMERALD CITY.

THIS ISN'T THE ROAD.

I KNOW, BUT WE HAVE LOST THE SCARECROW OVER THERE IN THE RIVER, AND ARE WONDERING HOW WE SHALL GET HIM AGAIN.

IF HE WASN'T SO BIG AND HEAVY I WOULD GET HIM FOR YOU.

HE ISN'T HEAVY A BIT, FOR HE IS STUFFED WITH STRAW. IF YOU'LL BRING HIM BACK, WE'LL THANK YOU EVER AND EVER SO MUCH.

WELL, I'LL TRY.

BUT IF I FIND HE IS TOO HEAVY TO CARRY I SHALL HAVE TO DROP HIM IN THE RIVER AGAIN.

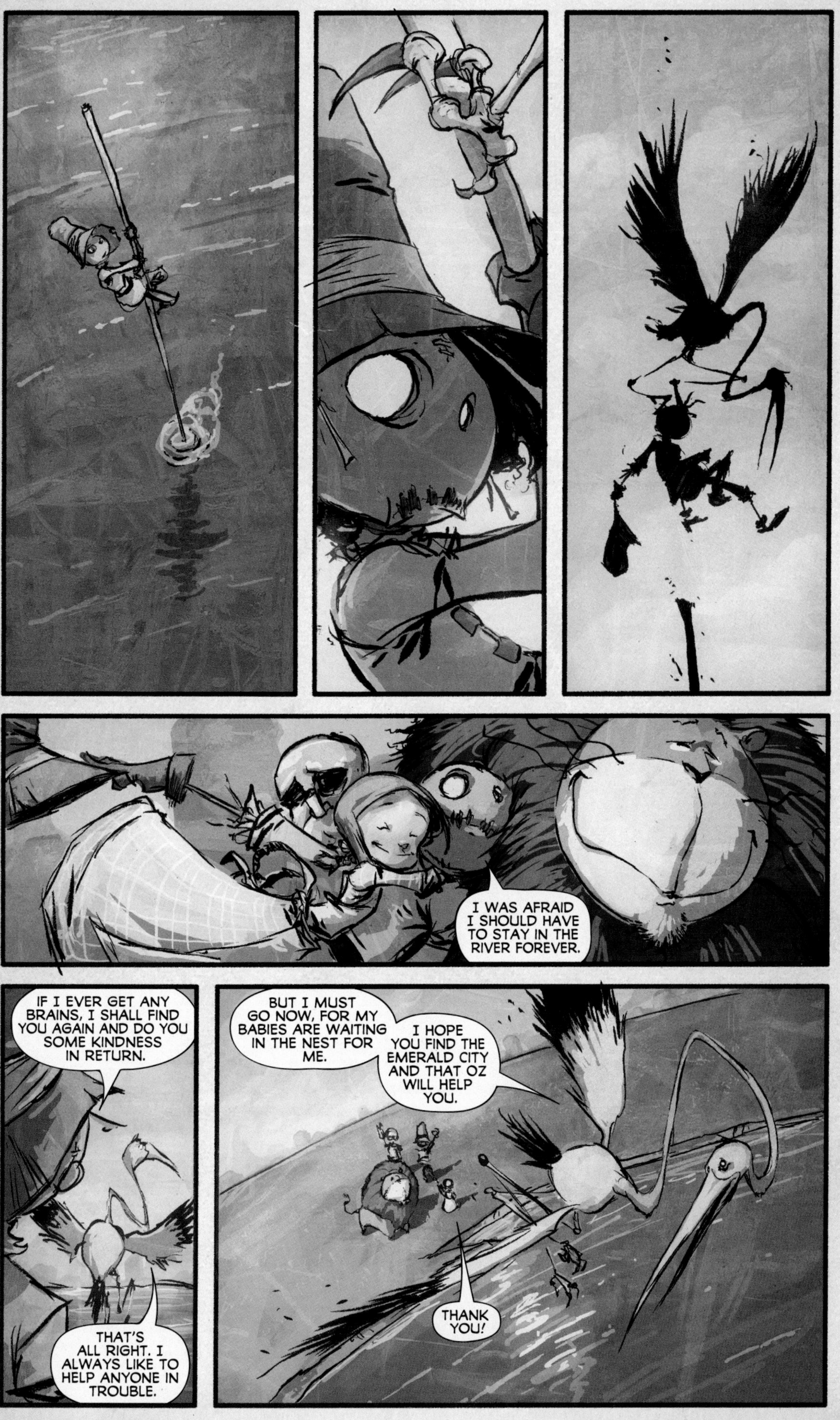
I WAS AFRAID I SHOULD HAVE TO STAY IN THE RIVER FOREVER.
IF I EVER GET ANY BRAINS, I SHALL FIND YOU AGAIN AND DO YOU SOME KINDNESS IN RETURN.
THAT'S ALL RIGHT. I ALWAYS LIKE TO HELP ANYONE IN TROUBLE.
BUT I MUST GO NOW, FOR MY BABIES ARE WAITING IN THE NEST FOR ME.
I HOPE YOU FIND THE EMERALD CITY AND THAT OZ WILL HELP YOU.
THANK YOU!

THEY WALKED ALONG LISTENING TO THE SINGING OF THE BIRDS AND LOOKING AT THE LOVELY FLOWERS.

AREN'T THEY BEAUTIFUL?

I SUPPOSE SO. WHEN I HAVE BRAINS I SHALL PROBABLY LIKE THEM BETTER.

I ALWAYS DID LIKE FLOWERS, THEY SEEM SO HELPLESS AND FRAIL.

IF I ONLY HAD A HEART, I SHOULD LOVE THEM.

BUT THERE ARE NONE IN THE FOREST SO BRIGHT AS THESE.

SOON THEY FOUND THEMSELVES IN THE MIDST OF A GREAT MEADOW OF POPPIES.

NOW WHEN THERE ARE MANY OF THESE FLOWERS TOGETHER THEIR ODOR IS SO POWERFUL THAT ANYONE WHO BREATHES IT FALLS ASLEEP.

IF THE SLEEPER IS NOT CARRIED AWAY FROM THE SCENT OF THE FLOWERS, HE SLEEPS ON AND ON FOREVER.

BUT DOROTHY DID NOT KNOW THIS.

I MUST SIT DOWN TO REST.

I WILL *NOT* LET YOU DO THAT.

WE MUST HURRY AND GET BACK TO THE ROAD OF YELLOW BRICK BEFORE DARK.

YES!

WHAT SHALL WE DO?

IF WE LEAVE HER HERE SHE'LL DIE... THE SMELL OF THE FLOWERS IS KILLING US... I MYSELF CAN SCARCELY KEEP MY EYES OPEN...

RUN FAST AND GET OUT OF THIS DEADLY FLOWER-BED AS SOON AS YOU CAN!

WE'LL BRING THE GIRL WITH US, BUT IF YOU SHOULD FALL ASLEEP YOU'RE TOO BIG TO BE CARRIED!

LET'S MAKE A CHAIR WITH OUR HANDS AND CARRY HER.

ON AND ON THEY WALKED. IT SEEMED THAT THE GREAT CARPET OF DEADLY FLOWERS WOULD NEVER END.

THE FLOWERS WERE TOO STRONG FOR HIM.

WE CAN DO NOTHING FOR HIM, FOR HE'S MUCH TOO HEAVY TO LIFT.

WE MUST LEAVE HIM HERE TO SLEEP ON FOREVER. PERHAPS HE'LL DREAM THAT HE HAS FOUND COURAGE AT LAST.

I'M SORRY -- THE LION WAS A VERY GOOD COMRADE FOR ONE SO COWARDLY.

WE CANNOT BE FAR FROM THE ROAD OF YELLOW BRICK NOW, FOR WE'VE COME NEARLY AS FAR AS THE RIVER CARRIED US AWAY.

GRRR

RROWRR!

*B*OUNDING OVER THE GRASS CAME A GREAT WILDCAT CHASING A FIELD-MOUSE.

ALTHOUGH THE TIN WOODMAN HAD NO HEART, HE KNEW IT WAS WRONG FOR THE WILDCAT TO TRY TO KILL SUCH A PRETTY, HARMLESS CREATURE.

THUK

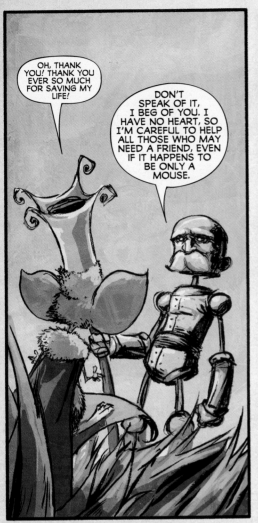

OH, THANK YOU! THANK YOU EVER SO MUCH FOR SAVING MY LIFE!

DON'T SPEAK OF IT, I BEG OF YOU. I HAVE NO HEART, SO I'M CAREFUL TO HELP ALL THOSE WHO MAY NEED A FRIEND, EVEN IF IT HAPPENS TO BE ONLY A MOUSE.

ONLY A MOUSE! WHY, I AM A QUEEN -- THE QUEEN OF ALL THE FIELD-MICE!

OH, INDEED.

THEREFORE YOU'VE DONE A GREAT DEED, AS WELL AS A BRAVE ONE, IN SAVING MY LIFE.

OH, YOUR MAJESTY! WE THOUGHT YOU WOULD BE KILLED!

HOW DID YOU MANAGE TO ESCAPE THE GREAT WILDCAT?

THIS FUNNY TIN MAN KILLED THE WILDCAT AND SAVED MY LIFE. SO HEREAFTER YOU MUST ALL SERVE HIM AND OBEY HIS SLIGHTEST WISH.

WE WILL!

ROWF!

COME BACK! COME BACK! TOTO SHALL NOT HURT YOU.

ARE YOU SURE HE WON'T BITE US?

I WON'T LET HIM, SO DON'T BE AFRAID.

IS THERE ANYTHING WE CAN DO TO REPAY YOU FOR SAVING THE LIFE OF OUR QUEEN?

NOTHING THAT I KNOW OF.

OH, YES! YOU CAN SAVE OUR FRIEND THE COWARDLY LION, WHO'S ASLEEP IN THE POPPY BED.

A LION! WHY, HE WOULD EAT US ALL UP!

OH, NO, THIS LION IS A COWARD. HE SAYS SO HIMSELF, AND HE WOULD NEVER HURT ANYONE WHO IS OUR FRIEND.

IF YOU'LL HELP US TO SAVE HIM I PROMISE HE SHALL TREAT YOU ALL WITH KINDNESS.

VERY WELL, WE'LL TRUST YOU. BUT WHAT SHALL WE DO?

ARE THERE MANY OF THESE MICE WHICH CALL YOU QUEEN AND ARE WILLING TO OBEY YOU?

YES, THERE ARE THOUSANDS.

THEN SEND FOR THEM ALL TO COME HERE AS SOON AS POSSIBLE, AND LET EACH ONE BRING A LONG PIECE OF STRING.

*T*HE QUEEN TOLD THE MICE TO GO AT ONCE AND GET ALL HER PEOPLE. AS SOON AS THEY HEARD HER ORDERS, THEY RAN AWAY IN EVERY DIRECTION.

NOW, YOU MUST GO TO THOSE TREES BY THE RIVERSIDE AND MAKE A TRUCK THAT WILL CARRY THE LION.

THE TIN WOODMAN WENT AT ONCE TO WORK.

SO FAST AND SO WELL DID HE WORK THAT BY THE TIME THE MICE BEGAN TO ARRIVE THE TRUCK WAS ALL READY FOR THEM.

ABOUT THIS TIME DOROTHY OPENED HER EYES.

PERMIT ME TO INTRODUCE TO YOU HER MAJESTY, THE QUEEN.

THE SCARECROW AND THE WOODMAN BEGAN TO FASTEN THE MICE TO THE TRUCK.

WHEN ALL THE MICE HAD BEEN HARNESSED, THEY WERE ABLE TO PULL IT QUITE EASILY TO THE PLACE WHERE THE LION LAY ASLEEP.

AFTER A GREAT DEAL OF HARD WORK, THE SCARECROW AND TIN WOODMAN MANAGED TO GET THE LION UP ON THE TRUCK.

THE QUEEN HURRIEDLY GAVE THE ORDER TO START, FOR SHE FEARED IF THE MICE STAYED AMONG THE POPPIES TOO LONG THEY ALSO WOULD FALL ASLEEP.

PULL!

AT FIRST THE LITTLE CREATURES, MANY THOUGH THEY WERE, COULD HARDLY STIR THE HEAVILY LOADED TRUCK.

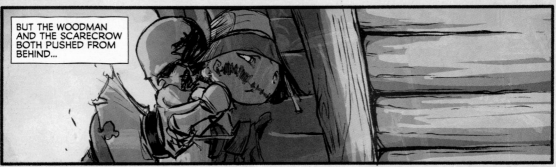

BUT THE WOODMAN AND THE SCARECROW BOTH PUSHED FROM BEHIND...

...AND THEY GOT ALONG BETTER.

THANK YOU! THANK YOU FOR SAVING HIM!

*T*HEN THE MICE WERE UNHARNESSED FROM THE TRUCK AND SCAMPERED AWAY TO THEIR HOMES.

IF YOU EVER NEED US AGAIN, COME OUT INTO THE FIELD AND BLOW THIS WHISTLE, AND WE SHALL HEAR YOU AND COME TO YOUR ASSISTANCE.

GOOD-BYE!

GOOD-BYE!

THEY SAT DOWN BESIDE THE LION...

...UNTIL HE SHOULD AWAKEN.